D1451264

For Amanda

STERLING CHILDREN'S BOOKS
New York

An Imprint of Sterling Publishing Co., Inc.
1166 Avenue of the Americas
New York, NY 10036

First Sterling edition published in 2019.
First published in the United Kingdom in 2018 by Pavilion Children's Books, 43 Great Ormond St, London WC1N 3HZ.

ISBN 978-1-4549-3418-9

Distributed in Canada by Sterling Publishing Co., Inc.
c/o Canadian Manda Group, 664 Annette Street
Toronto, Ontario M6S 2C8, Canada

For information about custom editions, special sales, and premium and corporate purchases,
please contact Sterling Special Sales at 800-805-5489 or specialsales@sterlingpublishing.com.

Manufactured in Canada
Lot #:
2 4 6 8 10 9 7 5 3
01/20

sterlingpublishing.com

The Five Positions

1

2

3

4

5

Ballet
Bunnies

Ballet
Bunnies

Lucy Freegard

STERLING CHILDREN'S BOOKS

New York

Betty's big ambition was to be a ballerina.

She danced all day and dreamed of being a star.

RUDOLPH CARROTYEV

But there was one
big problem.

Betty had never danced
on stage before.

She had only
danced for Bluebell.

Bluebell was Betty's baby sister,
and her BIGGEST fan.

She was very good at clapping.

Whenever they listened to music, Betty would dance.

She would pirouette in the bathroom,

twirl down the hallway,

and dart across the living room.

BALLET
BUNNIES

At home, Betty
felt unstoppable.

But at her dance class,
  things were different...

The end of class ballet show was coming up,

and Betty was feeling afraid.

She tried and tried,
but just couldn't remember the steps.

Everything was going wrong.

Unlike the other ballet
bunnies, Betty felt
very clumsy.

But even though she didn't always
get the dance moves right...

...she managed

to put

a SUPER

special

spin on them.

Thankfully, Betty's teacher could see the best
in all his students.

He made sure
that everyone
had fun in rehearsals

and a role in the show.

Betty practiced **really** hard to
make herself less nervous.

She stopped worrying about making a mistake, and she couldn't wait to share the stage with her friends!

BACKSTAGE

Best of all, Betty discovered she loved performing.

Especially for Bluebell, who was still Betty's biggest fan, and very good at wriggling, giggling, and of course…

After all, every little bunny who tries very hard
deserves **big** applause.